MW00958236

A Thistle Brook Book

The Mystery Hat

Written by
Rune Brandt Bennicke
& Jakob Hjort Jensen

Illustrated by
Jakob Hjort Jensen

Sky Pony Press
New York

Acknowledgments

The authors wish to thank Gabriele Pennacchioli for his invaluable input and guidance throughout the making of this book. Grazie, Maestro!

Thank you to our tireless agent, Jennifer Unter, for your perseverance and sticking-with-us-ness.

Finally, thank you to our wonderful editor at Sky Pony Press, Julie Matysik, for patiently correcting our terrible grammar.

Copyright © 2014 by Rune Brandt Bennicke and Jakob Hjort Jensen

All Rights Reserved. No part of this book may be reproduced in any manner without the express written consent of the publisher, except in the case of brief excerpts in critical reviews or articles. All inquiries should be addressed to
Sky Pony Press, 307 West 36th Street, 11th Floor, New York, NY 10018.

Sky Pony Press books may be purchased in bulk at special discounts for sales promotion, corporate gifts, fund-raising, or educational purposes. Special editions can also be created to specifications. For details, contact the Special Sales Department, Sky Pony Press, 307 West 36th Street, 11th Floor, New York, NY 10018 or info@ skyhorsepublishing.com.

Sky Pony® is a registered trademark of Skyhorse Publishing, Inc.®, a Delaware corporation.

Visit our website at www.skyponypress.com.

10 9 8 7 6 5 4 3 2 1

Manufactured in China, July 2014
This product conforms to CPSIA 2008

Library of Congress Cataloging-in-Publication Data

Bennicke, Rune Brandt, author.
The mystery hat / written by Rune Brandt Bennicke & Jakob Hjort Jensen ; illustrated by Jakob Hjort Jensen.
pages cm
Summary: "Crow, Pig, and Beaver are taking a nice stroll in the woods when they come across a red hat sitting in a puddle. Whose hat is it? What mysterious circumstances could have brought it to this very puddle?"-- Provided by publisher.
ISBN 978-1-62914-621-8 (hardback)
[1. Lost and found possessions--Fiction. 2. Animals--Fiction. 3. Friendship--Fiction. 4. Humorous stories.] I. Jensen, Jakob Hjort, author, illustrator. II. Title.
PZ7.B447112My 2014
[E]--dc23
2014021415

Cover illustrations by Jakob Hjort Jensen
Cover design by Danielle Ceccolini
Designed by Sara Kitchen

Ebook ISBN: 978-1-63220-220-8

To Benjamin, Ada & Emma

One sunny late-winter's morning, three friends were taking a stroll through the woods when they noticed something rather strange on the path just ahead of them.

"Watch out!" shrieked Crow.
"What happened here?"

A knitted hat lay in a small
puddle, all wet and soggy.

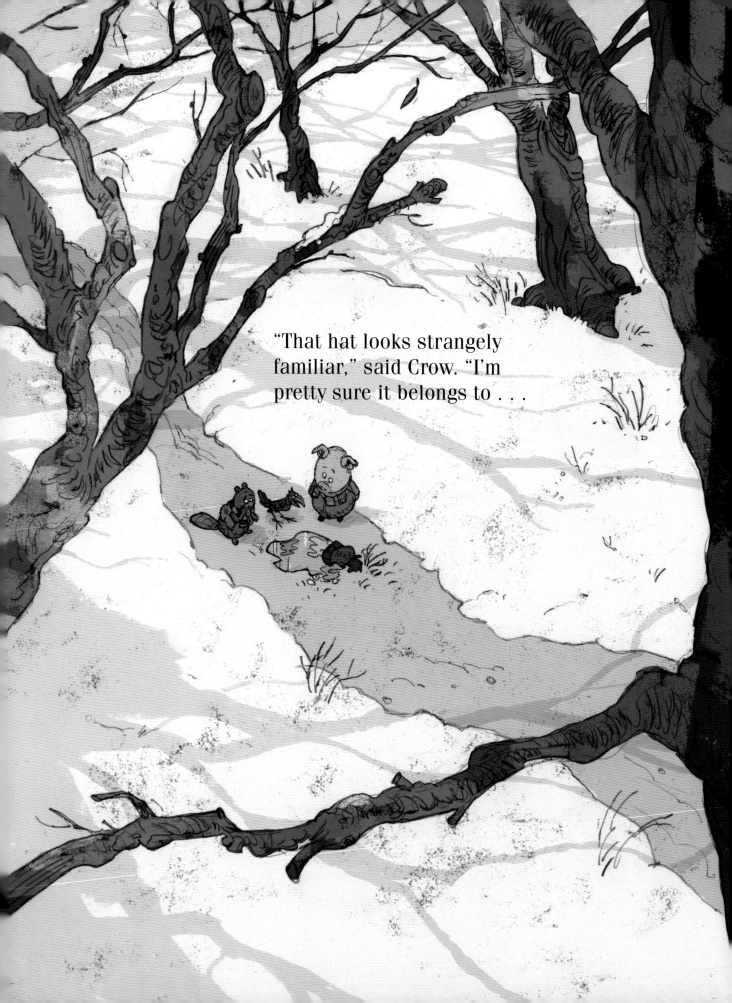

"That hat looks strangely familiar," said Crow. "I'm pretty sure it belongs to . . .

"He probably woke up early from his winter's sleep with his tummy rumbling and bumbling from hunger, so he hurried out to find something to eat.

"Seeing as he was still quite sleepy, he must not have seen the hole and SPLASH! SPLOOSH! down he fell, leaving only his hat!"

"And now he's sitting down there
waiting for someone to rescue him."

"QUICK! Let's find a rope and
pull poor Bear out at once!"

Pig took a little stick and poked it into the puddle.

"That's a very convincing story, Crow," he said. "But look. It's not deep enough to get much more than your feet wet, especially if you're a big bear."

"You're right! It's hogwash!" said Beaver. "Something awfully grim is going on here. In other words, something very bad!

"I don't know if you noticed, but as we passed the old farmhouse, the snowman out front wasn't there anymore."

"I once heard that the Snow People actually fly, especially if they're starving," shuddered Beaver.

"Perhaps the snowman was out hunting for supper!

"He must have spotted Turtle, who wears a hat just like this one. There he was, strutting along, minding his own business . . ."

". . . when SHWISHHHHHH, the
snowman grabbed Turtle, who must
have put up a fight, as you can tell
from the melted snowman-snow and
Turtle's hat," continued Beaver.

"If I know anything about snowmen it's that they love turtle soup. He's probably cooking up our little friend as we speak! We have to find him before he's turned into broth!"

Pig pondered for a while. Then he said, "Another interesting explanation, but I don't think it's very likely.

"You see, I just had breakfast with Turtle this morning. He's got a cold and isn't going anywhere. Look, you can see smoke coming out of his chimney."

"I think there's got to be a much simpler explanation to our little mystery." Pig took a moment to think really hard. Then it dawned on him!

He said, "Do you both remember when it snowed a lot a few days ago? It was very pretty. We all went outside to enjoy it, and then a snowball fight broke out."

"I almost hit you with a snowball, Crow, but you ducked and it took your hat right off instead.

"We thought you'd
lost it, but it must
have rolled
down this
hill where
after a while it
melted in the sun."

"I think we solved the mystery," smiled Pig. "It's *your* hat, silly Crow. It's still a bit wet, but you could try it on if you like."

"Well, what do you know? Of course, it's my hat! That's why it looked so familiar!" They all chuckled and giggled for quite some time.

Then they continued through the forest, looking for new adventures.

"Listen," said Pig. "Is that
our friend Bear I hear?"

"Oh, good!" sighed Crow.
"He got out, then!"

Beaver nodded in agreement.
"Perhaps the snowman
helped him. I'm so glad!"